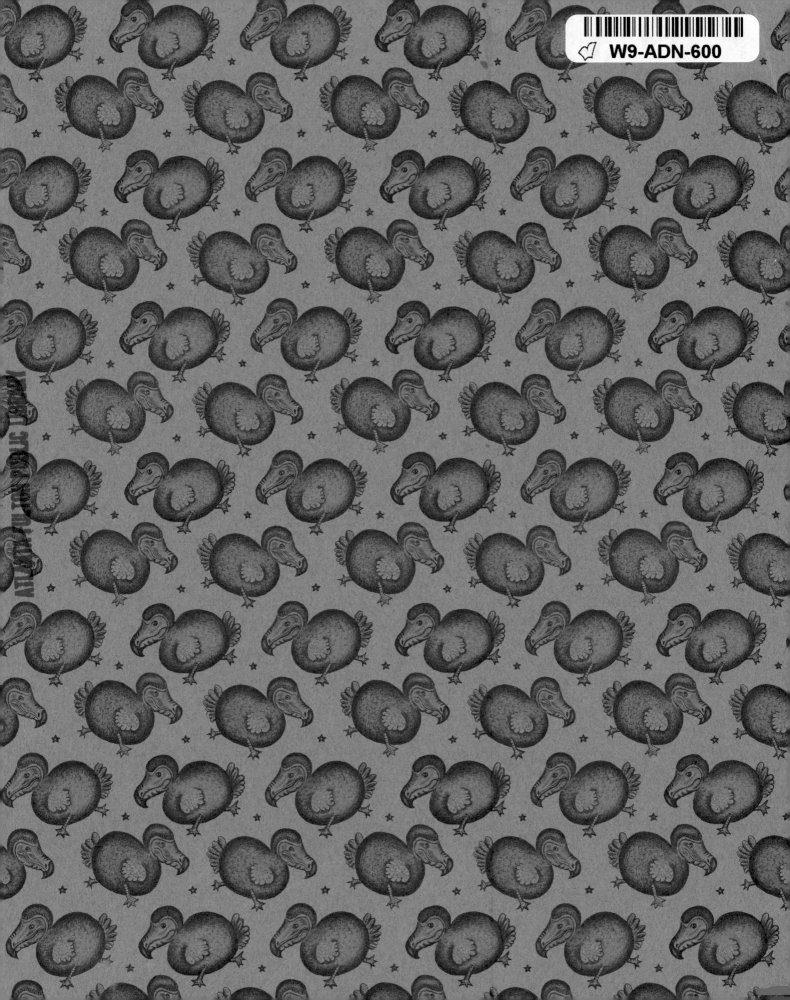

As Dead As A Dodo

With Illustrations by SHAWN RICE
And Text by
PAUL RICE & PETER MAYLE

David R. Godine, *Publisher*

BOSTON

FOR J.P.

First U.S. edition published in 1981 by
David R. Godine, Publisher, Inc.
306 Dartmouth Street
Boston, Massachusetts 02116

Text copyright © 1981 by Escargot Productions Ltd
Illustrations copyright © 1981 by Shawn Rice

Library of Congress Cataloging in Publication Data

Rice, Paul.
    As dead as a dodo.

    Summary: Describes sixteen extinct animals and explores
the reasons for their extinction. Also discusses presently
endangered species in the context of the indifferent attitude
people often have toward their environment.
    1. Extinct animals—Juvenile literature. 2. Wildlife con-
servation—Juvenile literature. [1. Extinct animals. 2.
Wildlife conservation]. I. Mayle, Peter. II. Rice, Shawn.
III. Title. QL88. R52 1981 591'.042 81-4062
ISBN 0-87923-401-6   AACR2

Contents

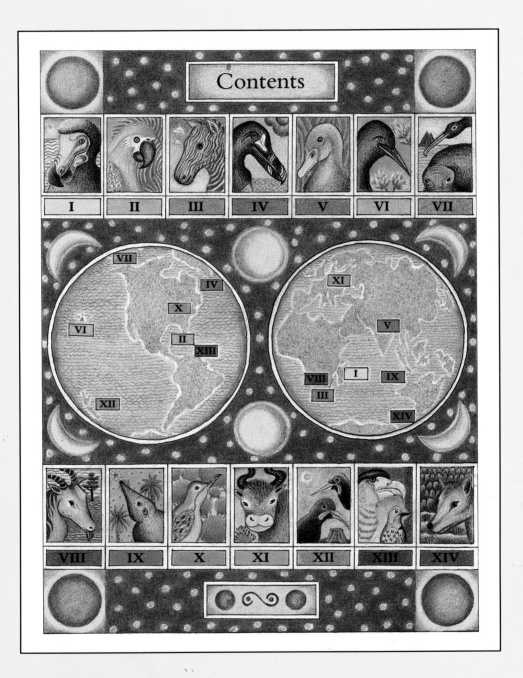

THE DODO
Raphus Cucullatus

 One of nature's less successful inventions, the Dodo lived on the island of Mauritius, in the Indian Ocean. It was a little bigger than a turkey. It was too stout to fly and couldn't even run without bumping its undercarriage on the ground. Its top speed was a brisk waddle.

When the Portuguese discovered Mauritius in the sixteenth century, they had never seen quite such a silly bird. They called it "doudo," which was Portuguese for simpleton.

The Dutch, who came to the island in 1598, thought the bird looked not only silly, but delicious. They promptly put Dodo on the menu.

The dogs, pigs, and rats that had come off the Dutch ships went to work on the Dodo's eggs, and within a hundred years the poor bird was eaten into extinction.

Not even one complete stuffed Dodo is left for us to see. All that remains is its distant relative, the pigeon. But just think how much more fun that statue in the park would be with a Dodo sitting on it.

THE CUBAN RED MACAW
Ara Tricolor

 The psittacidae family—parrots, macaws, and parakeets—has had an unfair share of casualties since the seventeenth century. At least twenty-eight known species have become extinct. The Cuban Red Macaw was one of them.

The macaws lived in pairs. Unlike most other birds, the male and female were the same color. They were small enough for two of them to squeeze into holes in palm trees, where they made their nests. They lived on fruit and seeds, and nobody has ever recorded finding a Cuban Red Macaw egg. We don't know much more than that about their habits.

What we do know is that their flesh was evil-smelling and unpleasant to taste. That obviously depended on how hungry you were, because the Cubans killed them for food. They were also killed as pests and captured for domestic pets. One way or another, they didn't stand much of a chance.

They disappeared in the late 19th century, proving that being harmless, evil-smelling, and bad-tasting is no guarantee of survival.

II

THE QUAGGA
Equus Quagga

If you can imagine a zebra who has forgotten to put on the bottom half of his striped pajamas, you have an idea of how the Quagga used to look.

These half-dressed horses grazed on the plains of southern Africa, where they had the odd habit of marching from one meal to the next in single file. To help them keep out of trouble, they often traveled with ostriches and white-tailed gnus. Between the three species, they could see, hear, or smell danger for miles around.

Sadly, even this arrangement wasn't enough to protect them from man. When the Dutch settled South Africa, they hunted throughout the plains and killed the Quagga for its skin and meat. They also adopted the African name, which was the closest humans could get to the shrill "khoua-khoua" of the Quagga's neigh.

A couple of Quaggas survived the voyage to London in the early 1800s, and their owner drove them in harness through Hyde Park. The local horses must have been astounded by these stripy foreigners.

Back in Africa, the herds became smaller and smaller, and the last wild Quagga was shot in 1870. A few lived on in zoos until the last Quagga of all, a rather elderly lady, died in Amsterdam on August 12th, 1883.

THE GREAT AUK
Pinguinus Impennis

This solemn-looking bird was originally called a penguin.
The birds we know today as penguins are hardly related
to the Auk at all, but were given the name because
of their similar style in evening dress.

The Auk was awkward on land, but much more at
home in the sea. It could dive to great depths, stay submerged longer
than a seal, and swim faster than man could row a boat. Only once
a year did it leave the water, to nest on the cold, rocky islands of the
North Atlantic. It produced just one egg a year, specially shaped to stop
it rolling out of the nest and differently marked so that each Auk
could recognise its own egg.

Man hunted the Auk from prehistoric times. Its flesh was good to
eat, its fat was used as fuel, its feathers stuffed many a bed, and its
collarbones were used as fish-hooks.

After centuries of being hunted, the remaining Auks gathered on a
tiny island off the tip of Iceland. As if they didn't have enough problems
their island home was destroyed in 1830 by an underwater volcano.

Fifty Auks survived. Museums became worried that they might
vanish without trace and in a burst of scientific enthusiasm paid to
have forty-eight birds killed for specimens.

Years later, a hundred Auks were found preserved in ice in
Newfoundland. But by then it was too late. The last two Auks in the
world had been killed in 1844 to add to a businessman's bird collection.

IV

THE INDIAN PINK-HEADED DUCK
Rhodonessa Caryophyllacea

 The shy and beautiful Pink-Headed Duck lived on the vast watery plains north of the Ganges river. By human standards, this was a high-risk neighborhood. Crocodiles infested the streams, and there was a large and thriving tiger population. Not surprisingly, the people population was small.

The Pink-Headed Duck seemed to like its own company. It lived alone for most of the year and paired only during the breeding season in April, building its nest in the middle of tufts of grass at the edges of small pools. The eggs were as beautiful as the birds: pale yellow or pure white and almost a perfect sphere in shape.

All was well in the ducks' quiet world until man started to cultivate the plains. Crops were raised and so were guns; the ducks were shot to sell in the food markets of Calcutta.

The last time anyone saw a wild specimen, or heard its soft, wheezy, whistling call, was in 1935. A few ducks survived in European zoos until the Second World War. Crocodiles and tigers may have been dangerous, but man proved to be fatal.

V

THE HAWAIIAN O-O
Moho Nobilis

Something about Hawaii in the past eighty years hasn't agreed with birds. More than twenty species have become extinct there since 1900.

The O-O had four problems, which were to prove fatal. It was beautiful. It was easy to hear, because its deep "took-took" cry carried for great distances. And it was easy to see sitting in a tree-top catching insects and sipping nectar with its whiskery tongue.

The fourth problem was a fashion among smart Hawaiians — wearing yellow and black feathered capes. Obviously, it took a lot of O-O's to cover one Hawaiian.

But worse was to come. The forests of Hawaii became smaller through felling, so there weren't as many tree-tops to sit in. And the demand for those wonderful yellow feathers grew as tourists started to buy them as souvenirs to take home.

While these honey-eaters have now gone, the feathered capes aren't yet extinct. One was sold in 1980 for £18,000 (about $40,000).

STELLER'S SEA-COW
Hydrodamalis Stelleri
THE SPECTACLED CORMORANT
Phalacrocorax Perspicillatus

 In 1741, the naturalist Georg Wilhelm Steller joined an expedition to find a land link between Asia and America. Instead, he discovered several strange and wonderful animals that man had never recorded seeing before.

The Sea-Cow was huge, often thirty feet long, with horny pads instead of teeth, a bristly chin, and tiny ears submerged in wrinkled skin. Birds perched on its back as it paddled along munching seaweed, lifting its head out of the water from time to time for a breath of air and a snort between mouthfuls. Often its head would be draped in seaweed, and from a long, long way away it might have been mistaken for a very portly mermaid with a green wig.

One of the Sea-Cow's neighbors was a large, handsome bird with rings of white skin round its eyes. Steller christened it the Spectacled Cormorant and described it as clumsy, slow-moving, and almost unable to fly—a distinct disadvantage for a bird.

Neither of these harmless creatures had any fear of man and provided countless meals for passing explorers and hunters. The Spectacled Cormorant disappeared sometime in the mid-1800s. The last recorded killing of a Sea-Cow was in 1768. Nobody sees mermaids in the Bering Sea any more.

VII

THE BLAAUBOK
Hippotragus Leucophaeus

 The "blue buck" belonged to the South African branch of the antelope family. A few of its relatives, like the roan and the sable, still live in Africa today.

Some people called it "the blue goat", but it was really far too well-dressed for a goat. Standing about four feet high at the shoulder, it was an elegant creature with a most marvelously colored blue-gray coat that looked like thick velvet. A curious thing about the Blaaubok was that it actually changed color after death, the coat fading to an ordinary dull gray.

It was as good to eat as it was to look at. When the Dutch came to South Africa at the end of the seventeenth century, it didn't take them long to develop a taste for Blaaubok meat. Unfortunately, the settlers were excellent shots, and the "blue buck" had the sad distinction of being the first African mammal to be completely wiped out by the gun.

There may have been a second type of Blaaubok, with shorter hair and no mane or beard, but this was never confirmed. In fact, the species was killed off so quickly that people hardly had time to know of its existence before it was gone.

VIII

THE CHRISTMAS ISLAND MUSK-SHREW
Crocidura Fuliginosa Trichura

 The Christmas Island Musk-Shrew disappeared mysteriously in the space of eight years. Despite being called a "musk-shrew", it belongs to a different group of small animals—the white-toothed shrews.

They lived on an island in the Indian Ocean that was discovered on Christmas Day, 1643. Nobody bothered them for more than two hundred years, and until 1900 the colony of Musk-Shrews still made up the main part of the island's population.

That year, man inhabited the island, and a visitor wrote: "This little animal is extremely common all over the island, and at night its shrill squeak like the cry of a bat can be heard on all sides. It lives in holes in rocks and roots of trees and seems to feed mainly on small beetles."

Eight years after this was written, the Musk-Shrew had vanished. An expedition in 1908 searched the whole island without hearing a single squeak. And nobody knows why.

Those small beetles that the Musk-Shrew fed on could hardly have learned to fight back. Perhaps the domestic cats that were brought to the island lived on a diet of Musk-Shrew for several years. Or perhaps man and his animals brought some fatal disease to the island.

Whatever happened, there are no more happy Christmases for the Musk-Shrew.

IX

THE PASSENGER PIGEON
Ectopistes Migratorius

 When the first European explorers came to North America, they could hardly believe the abundance and variety of the bird population. Even more unbelievable were the numbers of this single species.

More than a third of all the birds in America were Passenger Pigeons. Each summer, they nested in the northern forests; each winter, they flew south. Not in hundreds or thousands, but in millions.

At nesting time, up to ninety square miles of forest could be packed with pigeons. You could hear a nesting flock several miles away. And when the birds flew overhead they blotted out the sun and filled the air with a noise like a tornado. One naturalist saw a flock that he estimated was a mile wide and 240 miles long—more than two thousand million birds.

It was impossible to imagine them ever becoming extinct. They were shot, trapped with nets, even knocked from branches with poles and clubs. One professional hunter claimed to kill more than 10,000 pigeons a day. The supply of pigeon meat seemed endless.

It wasn't. During the 19th century, the hungry American population jumped from five million to seventy-six million. At the same time whole forests were vanishing. The pigeons' breeding cycle was upset. Their food became scarcer.

Around the turn of the century, the last wild pigeon was shot in Canada. The sole survivor of the species was Martha, who was born and raised in the Cincinnati Zoo. She attracted visitors from all over the world until she died on September 1st, 1914. She was twenty-nine.

X

THE AUROCHS
Bos Primigenius

 The cave dwellers of Lascaux decorated their walls with paintings of the Aurochs, and Julius Caesar wrote about it.

It was a difficult animal to ignore — an ox almost the size of an elephant. It stood about seven feet high and often measured eight feet across from the tip of one horn to the other.

Most animals wisely left the Aurochs alone as it plodded through the forests of Europe and the near East. Even wolves had second thoughts about those eight-foot horns.

To man, though, the Aurochs looked like a giant supply of steak. And among the German nobility, a silver-rimmed Aurochs horn was the most elegant kind of drinking mug to have at banquets.

The huge ox began to disappear as the European forests were cut down. A herd of thirty head was known to survive in 1565 on a game reserve in Poland, and laws were passed to protect them. That didn't stop poachers, who took the remaining animals one by one. The last Aurochs died in 1627.

Cattle experts have been trying to recreate the species by careful breeding. One day they might come close, but it is unlikely there will ever be another Aurochs. The nearest thing we're likely to see is one of its small descendants, the Spanish fighting bull.

THE HUIA
Heteralocha Acutirostris

 No matter how busy they were during the rest of the day, the Huia bird and his mate always ate together, and for a most remarkable reason.

They lived in the forests of New Zealand, and their favorite food, a large grub called the Hu-Hu, lived in the trunks of decaying trees. To get the Hu-Hu out of the tree trunk and into the stomach, the birds had to crack the bark before picking out the insect.

The male bird, with his short, chisel-shaped bill, would hammer away at the trunk. The female, with her long, tweezer-shaped bill, was then able to pick the insect out. Neither bird could survive alone. Together, they were nature's answer to the knife and fork.

Despite this ingenious team work, the Huia gradually died out as the forests were cleared and suitable homes became more difficult to find. New bird diseases came into the country when the mynah bird arrived in New Zealand, and they may have speeded up the process of extinction.

Huia birds were last seen in 1907. It would be nice to think that they were having a specially good lunch.

THE GUADALOUPE CARACARA
Caracara Lutosa
THE RED-SHAFTED FLICKER
Colaptes Cafer Rufipileus

 Most species that man has made extinct were destroyed through thoughtlessness or accident. The Caracara was exterminated on purpose.

It was a brown hawk, once the biggest and possibly the loudest bird on the island of Guadaloupe. It gabbled when fighting and screamed when surprised. Each spring, it settled on the cliffs, produced a family of three in its stick-and-cactus nest, and went about its noisy way.

A long-legged carrion-eater, its diet was mixed: small birds, shellfish, mice, insects, and the occasional dead goat. This fondness for goat's meat led to extinction. The Guadaloupe goat-herders, convinced that the bird was stealing goat kids, had shot or poisoned every Caracara on the island by 1900.

Their goats then proceeded to help in the extinction of another island bird, a large woodpecker with the wonderful name of the Red-Shafted Flicker. The Flicker lived in the cypress groves until the goats came and literally ate it out of house and home by chewing up the groves.

By 1906, the Red-Shafted Flicker population was down to forty. The man who counted them so carefully then shot twelve of them for museum specimens. Live Flickers were never seen again on Guadaloupe.

XIII

THE TASMANIAN WOLF
Thylacinus Cynocephalus

 At one time, the Tasmanian Wolf could be found all over Australia and New Guinea. It retreated about three thousand years ago, when a better-equipped competitor called the dingo came into its territory. The island of Tasmania was free of dingos and offered an easier life. The Wolves stayed there.

The Wolf was about six feet long from snout to tail. It was a marsupial, so the babies were tucked in a pouch beneath their mother's belly. The pouch faced backwards, to protect the young from bumps when going through the bush.

Tasmanian Wolves ate meat. They did their hunting by night, preying on small marsupials and birds with a fearsome set of teeth and jaws that opened nearly 180 degrees. They were unpopular with sheep-farmers and even less popular with sheep.

The farmers steadily killed off the Tasmanian Wolf until 1930, when the last wild specimen was shot. Three years later, the last captive specimen died in Hobart Zoo. Four years after that, the Tasmanian Government placed the Tasmanian Wolf on the list of protected animals.

Since then, a few people have reported seeing Tasmanian Wolves, but none of the sightings has been confirmed. We can but hope.

Shawn Rice's original works of art
are exhibited exclusively by
Portal Gallery Ltd., London, England.

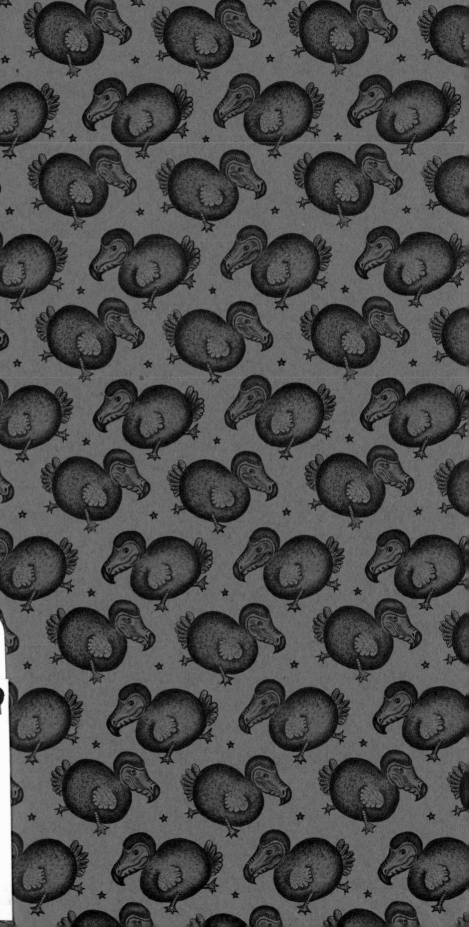